THE WONDERFUL WORLD OF WORDS

11

Constable Word Investigates

Dr Lubna Alsagoff
PhD (Stanford)

Marshall Cavendish Children

He loved to work on word puzzles when he was free.

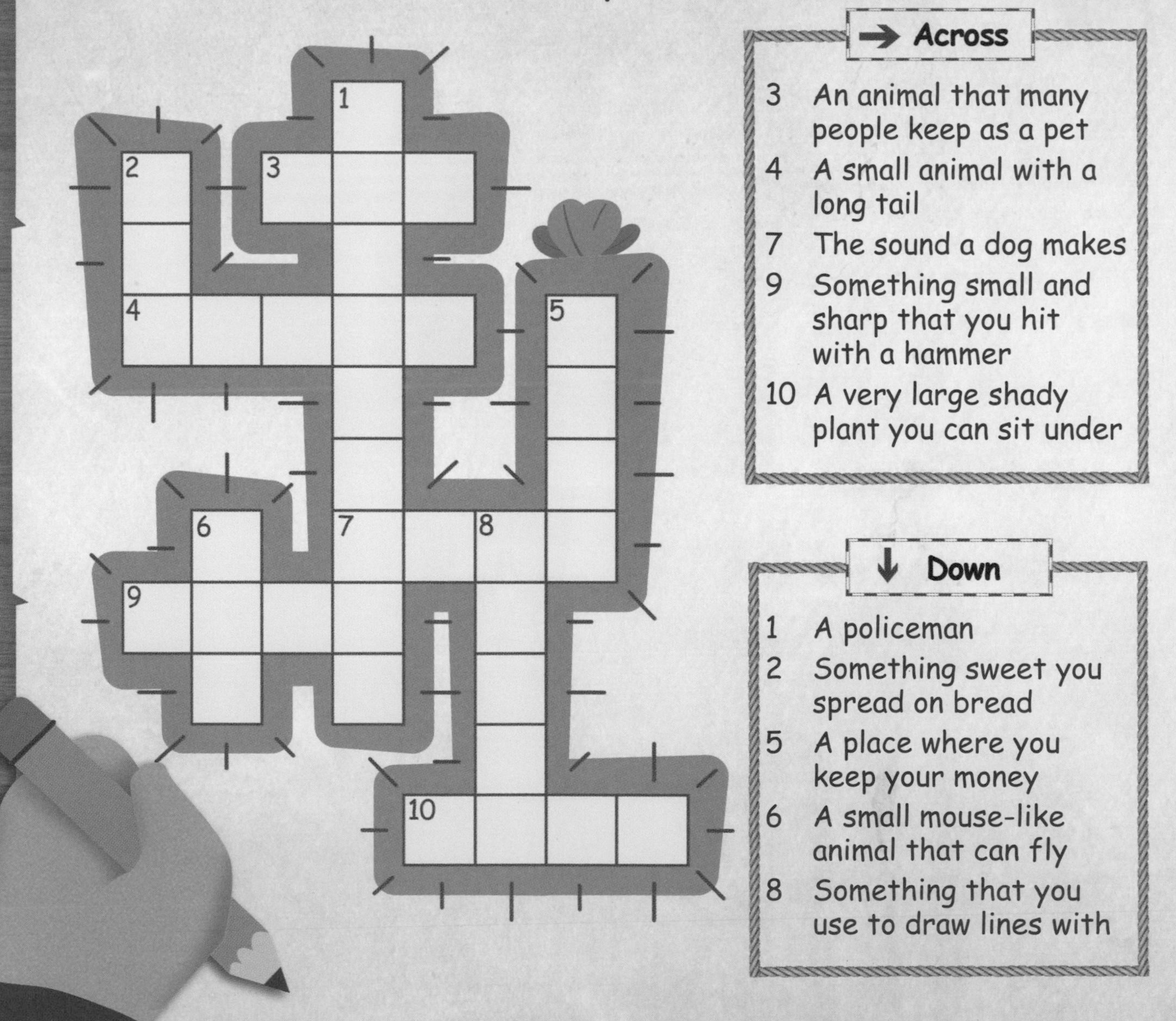

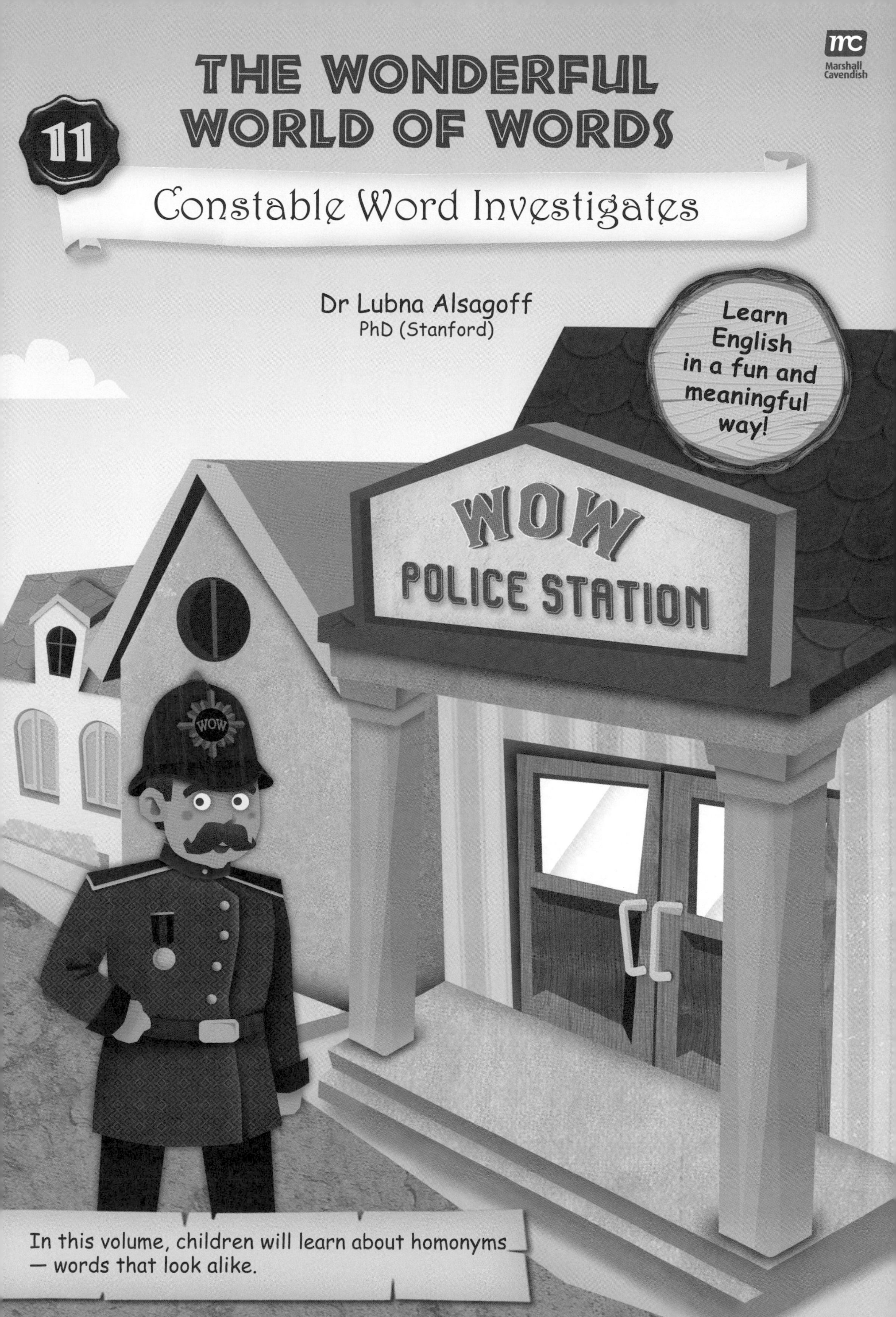
mc
Marshall Cavendish
THE WONDERFUL WORLD OF WORDS
11
Constable Word Investigates
Dr Lubna Alsagoff
PhD (Stanford)
Learn English in a fun and meaningful way!
WOW
POLICE STATION
WOW
In this volume, children will learn about homonyms — words that look alike.

Other Titles in the

Wonderful World of Words (WOW) Series

When the constable was about to start on a puzzle, the phone rang! It was the WOW bank manager. He needed help.

Just as Constable Word was about to leave, the phone rang again!

And again!

And again!

Strange things seemed to be happening in the town of WOW.

At the WOW bank, three men
were trying to catch some fish!

Come back here, Toby!
In another part of town, a woman was frantically running after her dog.
In a park nearby, a man was frightened by a tree!
Woof! Woof!

In school, the children wondered why a bat was flying across the baseball field.

At the nail salon, Lucy did not know what to do with the bags of nails someone had brought.

Mrs Mouse wondered why her husband wasn't home. He said he was stuck in a jam.

Amelia was struggling to draw
straight lines for her math homework.

Hello, Amelia,
did you ask for me?

There was something missing from Billy's desk.
Online
Learning
More Details
Eek!

Gentlemen, you can't fish in a bank!
$
WOW BANK
River Street
We're sorry, Constable. We wanted to fish at the bank of the river.
No, gentlemen, this is the bank at River Street!
$
WOW
River Street
bank
riverbank

Toby, let me
have that, please.
Woof!
Woof!
BARK
the outer layer of a
the sound that a
makes

BAT

A stick with a handle that players use to hit balls with.

BAT

A flying a _ _ _ _ _ that looks like a mouse, but has w _ _ _ s and feeds at night.

WOW
NAILS

WOW
traffic jam
jam

ruler
mouse
ruler
mouse

The Fabulous Forest of WOW

In the Forest of WOW, Princess Preposition told Owl, Rabbit and Squirrel about the royal family who lived in the kingdom of WOW.

King Noun
Queen Verb
Prince Pronoun
Artisan Adverb
Admiral Adjective
Princess Preposition
Ari Article
Count Quantifier

NOUN

King Noun looks after words called nouns. These words name things, people, animals and places.

VERB

Queen Verb looks after words called verbs. These words name actions or describe a state of things.

ADJECTIVE
bright
angry
tired
Admiral Adjective takes care of words called adjectives. These words describe how things, people or places look or feel.
ADVERB
sadly
happily
carefully
Artisan Adverb looks after words called adverbs. These words describe how, when or where an action or event takes place.

QUANTIFIER

one two many much few twenty

Count Quantifier helps the king count all his nouns.

ARTICLE

the

Ari Article looks after the small but important words that usually come before nouns, like *a*, *an* or *the*.

PRONOUN

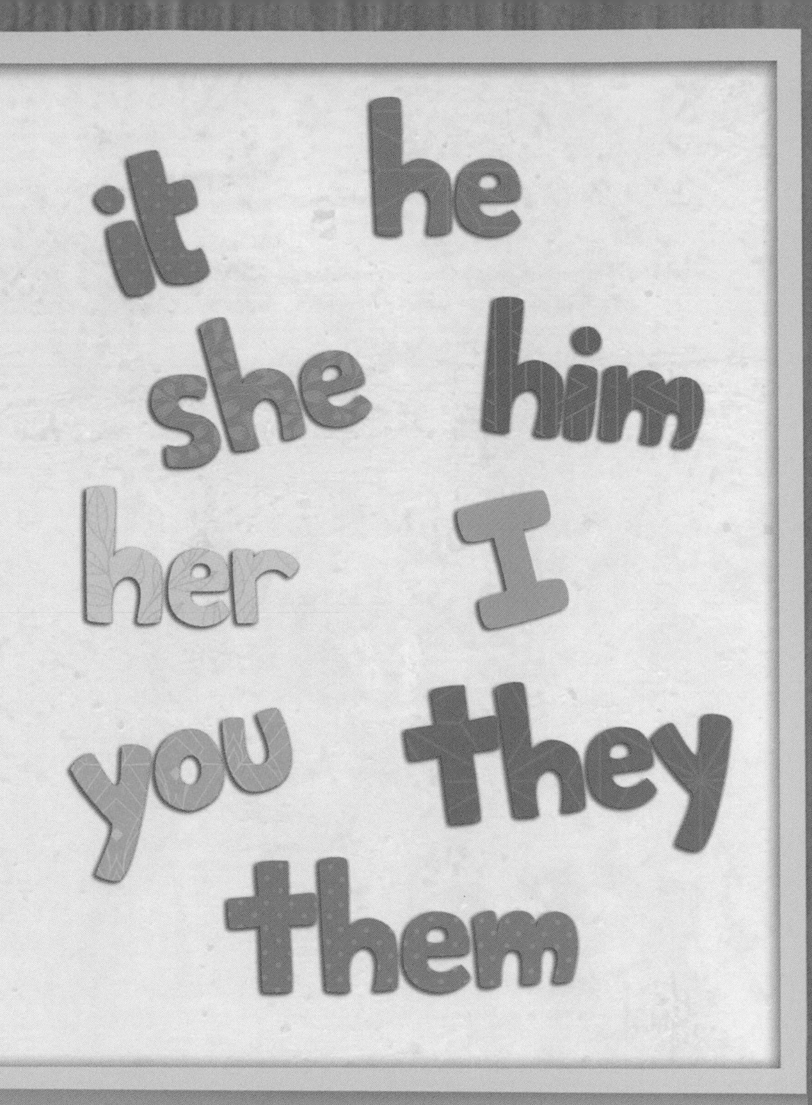

Prince Pronoun is in charge of pronouns. These are words that stand in place of nouns.

PREPOSITION

Princess Preposition looks after words called prepositions. These words tell us about time and place.

Many strange things happened in WOW today.

Constable Word told three fishermen that they had to fish at the riverbank and not at the bank in River Street.

A tree was barking at a frightened man, while a dog was happily walking around the park with a piece of bark in its mouth!

The children could finally play baseball once more!

Billy's mother stood helplessly on a chair when she saw a large mouse in her living room. Billy had to use the computer without his mouse!

Look for these words in the newspaper article.
Circle the correct word class.

	Word								
1	three	noun	verb	adjective	adverb	pronoun	preposition	quantifier	article
2	fishermen	noun	verb	adjective	adverb	pronoun	preposition	quantifier	article
3	they	noun	verb	adjective	adverb	pronoun	preposition	quantifier	article
4	fish	noun	verb	adjective	adverb	pronoun	preposition	quantifier	article
5	the	noun	verb	adjective	adverb	pronoun	preposition	quantifier	article
6	in	noun	verb	adjective	adverb	pronoun	preposition	quantifier	article
7	tree	noun	verb	adjective	adverb	pronoun	preposition	quantifier	article
8	barking	noun	verb	adjective	adverb	pronoun	preposition	quantifier	article
9	frightened	noun	verb	adjective	adverb	pronoun	preposition	quantifier	article
10	happily	noun	verb	adjective	adverb	pronoun	preposition	quantifier	article
11	around	noun	verb	adjective	adverb	pronoun	preposition	quantifier	article
12	bark	noun	verb	adjective	adverb	pronoun	preposition	quantifier	article
13	helplessly	noun	verb	adjective	adverb	pronoun	preposition	quantifier	article
14	a	noun	verb	adjective	adverb	pronoun	preposition	quantifier	article
15	she	noun	verb	adjective	adverb	pronoun	preposition	quantifier	article
16	large	noun	verb	adjective	adverb	pronoun	preposition	quantifier	article
17	without	noun	verb	adjective	adverb	pronoun	preposition	quantifier	article
18	children	noun	verb	adjective	adverb	pronoun	preposition	quantifier	article
19	finally	noun	verb	adjective	adverb	pronoun	preposition	quantifier	article
20	play	noun	verb	adjective	adverb	pronoun	preposition	quantifier	article

Dear Parents,

In this volume, children learn about homonyms through a series of funny events that happen in the kingdom of WOW. Homonyms are words that look alike — they have the same form — but have different meanings.

In the forest of WOW, the animals learn about the royal family and how words are categorised into different word classes.

Page Possible Answers

2

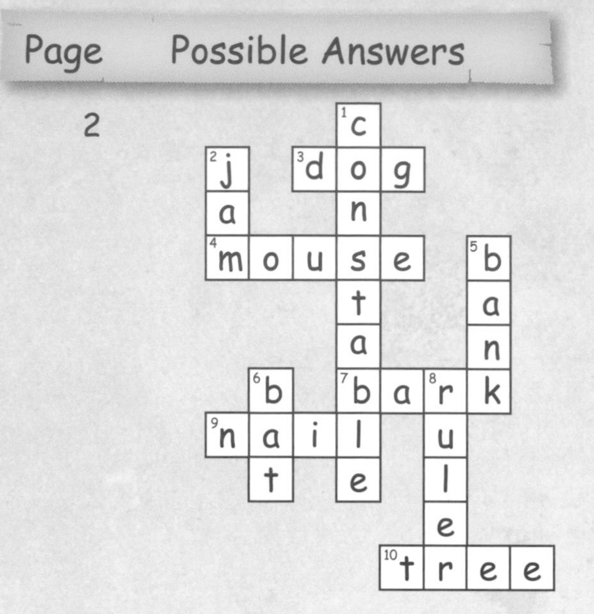

11 tree, dog

12 animal, wings

23

	Word								
1	**three**	noun	verb	adjective	adverb	pronoun	preposition	**quantifier**	article
2	**fishermen**	**noun**	verb	adjective	adverb	pronoun	preposition	quantifier	article
3	**they**	noun	verb	adjective	adverb	**pronoun**	preposition	quantifier	article
4	**fish**	noun	**verb**	adjective	adverb	pronoun	preposition	quantifier	article
5	**the**	noun	verb	adjective	adverb	pronoun	preposition	quantifier	**article**
6	**in**	noun	verb	adjective	adverb	pronoun	**preposition**	quantifier	article
7	**tree**	**noun**	verb	adjective	adverb	pronoun	preposition	quantifier	article
8	**barking**	noun	**verb**	adjective	adverb	pronoun	preposition	quantifier	article
9	**frightened**	noun	verb	**adjective**	adverb	pronoun	preposition	quantifier	article
10	**happily**	noun	verb	adjective	**adverb**	pronoun	preposition	quantifier	article
11	**around**	noun	verb	adjective	adverb	pronoun	**preposition**	quantifier	article
12	**bark**	**noun**	verb	adjective	adverb	pronoun	preposition	quantifier	article
13	**helplessly**	noun	verb	adjective	**adverb**	pronoun	preposition	quantifier	article
14	**a**	noun	verb	adjective	adverb	pronoun	preposition	quantifier	**article**
15	**she**	noun	verb	adjective	adverb	**pronoun**	preposition	quantifier	article
16	**large**	noun	verb	**adjective**	adverb	pronoun	preposition	quantifier	article
17	**without**	noun	verb	adjective	adverb	pronoun	**preposition**	quantifier	article
18	**children**	**noun**	verb	adjective	adverb	pronoun	preposition	quantifier	article
19	**finally**	noun	verb	adjective	**adverb**	pronoun	preposition	quantifier	article
20	**play**	noun	**verb**	adjective	adverb	pronoun	preposition	quantifier	article

CERTIFICATE
OF ACHIEVEMENT
WOW
Volume 11
Awarded to
Name ____________________
for mastering Volume 11
Date ________________

Welcome to the **Wonderful World of Words (WOW)**!

This series of books aims to help children learn English grammar in a fun and meaningful way through stories.

Children will read and discover how the people and animals of WOW learn the importance of grammar, as the adventure unfolds from volume to volume.

What's Inside

Imaginative stories that engage children, and help develop an interest in learning grammar	Adventures that encourage children to learn and understand grammar, and not just memorise rules	Games and activities to reinforce learning and check for understanding

About the Author

Dr Lubna Alsagoff is a language educator who is especially known for her work in improving the teaching of grammar in schools and in teacher education. She was Head of English Language and Literature at the National Institute of Education (NIE), and has published a number of grammar resources used by teachers and students. She has a PhD in Linguistics from Stanford University, USA, and has been teaching and researching English grammar for over 30 years.

Published by Marshall Cavendish Children
An imprint of Marshall Cavendish International

Printed in Singapore

visit our website at:
www.marshallcavendish.com